T0157980

MASTER OF
MANHATTAN
You Lose Or Win

Jeffrey Bonds

authorHOUSE®

AuthorHouse™
1663 Liberty Drive
Bloomington, IN 47403
www.authorhouse.com
Phone: 1-800-839-8640

First published by AuthorHouse 3/22/2011

ISBN: 978-1-4567-5846-2 (sc)
ISBN: 978-1-4567-5845-5 (e)

Library of Congress Control Number: 2011904892

Printed in the United States of America

She was in the middle. Martha Manhattan met a man. He was a killer of an ink pen. In other words he was a writer. The killer of an ink pen was merely a writer trying to make it in the big times. The writer Jeffries Lagheart was just trying to convince Martha that he was the right one for her. The time was right. There was more than opportunity in New York. There was fun and enjoyment. There were money, businesses and jobs there. What more could a writer ask for? Jeffries Lagheart saw with an advantage to take New York by storm. That's what he'd do.

Manhattan was as beautiful as could be, and love was not the only thing that she was looking for. It was her past. Something was missing.

She had built a wall around herself after her Mother Karen Manhattan had gotten badly sick. It was the year of October. 3, 2003 in New York in a big town called Manhattan. The city of Manhattan was bought and owned by the family called the Manhattans. Ted Manhattan was the big man. It had been past down to him by his father,

James Manhattan. The legacy lived on and now was there a problem to face.

Joe Holmes was the problem. He was a big time drug dealer and was trying to take over Manhattan. Ted Manhattan would never let that happen. He had too much money, power, position, and he was too hard hearted. Ted had sent some of his men to warn Joe Holmes that if he didn't stop making trouble in his town he was going to hang him dead. But Joe Holmes was convinced that he was going to take over Manhattan.

Holmes was big hearted and knew that Ted Manhattan meant business, but he had too much to gain than to stop now. He wanted to rule Manhattan. He had a great plan and a great chance to do just that. It was not Joe Holmes money that would give him Manhattan. It was his brains and wits. Holmes was drawing up maps of plans to do what and when to do it. Yet, one thing was standing in the way. His father's antique watch that Ted Manhattan's family. When gotten that. The city was all his.

The city then would be ran by drug dealers instead of Catholic's Hood people. Ted Manhattan had heard news about Joe Holmes. Yet it didn't put fear in his heart. He was about to do a tiling that Manhattan would never forget. It was to serve Joe Holmes right. It was a while when there was a ring at Joe Holmes telephone. It was Ted Manhattan.

"Hello? This is Joe Holmes. How may I help you?" said Holmes with a questioning voice.

"Get out of town..."

Then there was a busy tone it was as if it was the end of the world for Holmes. He had never felt like this before. He was afraid and terrified. Then one of his men saw that look on his face and knew that he was at panic.

At the Manhattan's it was not so quiet fainting. Martha saw the look on her father's face that he had the look as if he'd made a wise decision. She wanted to know just what did he do? Had he received victory? If so what would he do next?

"Father?" said Martha with a concern. "You look as though you are worried about something?"

"Me?"

"Yes, now you've got me worried," she replied with a deep concern.

"Well there's not a thing to worry about Martha," said Ted Manhattan as to be full of confidence. "We just say that I got rid of nothing but trouble."

"Trouble? Who's giving us trouble?" asked Martha. "Father is there something that you are not telling me?"

"Well Martha if you really want'na know I just told Joe Holmes to leave the city." replied Ted Manhattan. "He's been causing us nothing but trouble. So for the city's best benefit he must get out of the city Martha."

"Father you couldn't have?" she shouts with a low lady like voice. "You can't be telling the truth?"

"Why do you say that?" he demanded an explanation." Why Martha your light black American skin completion has totally changed to red. You look as if you are on fire. What's this nonsense?"

Martha then ran into another room. She was angry. Something was on her mind. Ted Manhattan was a bit disappointed. He had no idea that she would take it so hard. And the question was why? What did she have to gain from Joe Holme? Had she been talking to him? No there must had been some other explanation. Or could it had been a money bargain between the two? Ted Manhattan would find the answer and find it soon.

Martha came running out the door. She was angry. She had her clothing packed. She was leaving Manhattan. She said that she would never come back. Ted hated it what was up between Martha and Joe Holmes? He couldn't figure it out. By now he was more than sure that Joe Holmes had to leave town now. Then Ted found himself questioning Martha.

"So you are leaving?"

"Yes." replied Martha. "I am tired of Manhattan Father. I've had enough."

"You know you haven't given me a reason?" Ted said as he brought out his wallet. "Here here's a check take it with you you might need it?"

"Oh Father I don't need your money. You keep it I can make it on my own." she led the check on a table that looked as if it was worth at least several thousands of dollars.

He then swaded his head. That was just like Martha. She was not going to accept any help because when she had made up her mind she had made up her mind. Ted knew that there was no chance that she was going to accept his offer.

"So you are always going to be the same old Martha aren't you?" he said as to be proud of his daughter. "Well what can I say? Take care?"

She was just as pretty as could be. She then grabbed her luggage and headed for the doors. She was Martha and all she thought about was the fact that her father had told Joe Holmes to leave town. Holmes had something planned. Had this been one of his plans to get Martha to leave home? Could Holmes had been that dirty? It was about two o'clock a.m. The house began to just notice how lonely it was without Martha.

"Ted?" Karen Manhattan pleaded. "My you look as though you are stoned sad? What's wrong?"

"It Martha she has just left." Replied Ted Manhattan. "She got upset because I told her that I told Joe Holmes to leave town."

"My goodness..." exclaimed Karen.

"Yes, she seemed very upset. For what is very unknown to me." He said with a deep concern. "I should had known that Holmes was up to something. Why that dirty rat."

"Just what's your point Ted?"

"Why this is probably one of his dirty plans." Responded Ted Manhattan as wanting to do away with Joe Holmes, "What that man has stole my very daughter."

"Oh Ted that could had happened." Said Karen Manhattan.

"Well what other excuse could there be Karen?" asked Ted with a voice in demand. "I am just out of reasons there Karen."

"I don't know." Karen said back to him. "I don't know."

It was not long before Ted Manhattan had gotten on the phone. He'd called Framey Barker, one of his men. Framey was his main hit man. He knew that if anyone could get the job done it was Framey Barker. There the phone began to ring.

"Hello you have reached Framey Barker's place may I help you?" said one of Framey's men.

"Yes Dexter let me speak to Framey please?" said Ted Manhattan. "This is very important Dexter."

"Ok, Boss."

"Hello Ted what's up. Is there trouble?" said Framey.

"Quiet much Framey. Quiet much." Replied Ted.

"So tell me about it Boss?" said Framey.

"Look someone's got'ta take care of Joe Holmes. He's somehow convinced Martha to leave home." Said Ted Manhattan as to mean business. " Look I need you to take care of him."

"How soon, Boss?"

"Now Framey, I need you to take care of him now

before he gets too far. He has already done enough damage." Said Ted Manhattan. "I can't wait a minute longer."

"Ok I'll be right over, Boss." Replied Framey Barker as to waste no time. "He's done with Boss."

It was not long before the phone was dead. It was not long before the men at Framey's had seen him grab his coat and head for the door. They knew that when Framey had that type of look on his face he meant business. They all stared to move in haste and followed Framey Barker. It was not long before the cars had started. That's when the killer of an ink pen came in the picture. Jeffries Lagheart was that killer of an ink pen. He had been writing the story of a life time, but when he'd laid eyes on Martha he'd known that she was the most beautiful lady that he'd ever seen.

She was the age of thirty and had the light skin complexion of a very light skinned color of a black woman. Her sin was smooth. She stood about six foot tall. She looked very, very intelligent. She carried herself very well mannered. It was not long at dark night that he'd bumped into Martha.

"Excuse me?" said Jeffries Lagheart.

"Why excuse me," replied Martha.

"Why it was all my mistake, I shouldn't had bumped into you. Please pardon me." Said Jeffries Lagheart." I just get clumsy sometimes I'm terribly sorry."

"Well you just completely insist that it's your fault." Said she. "But you seem to be such a gentleman."

Then she'd picked up her pocket book. She started on her way. Jeffreies Lagheart then interrupted her. She seemed like such an interested person. She seemed like such a lady. He wanted to get to know her. He then spoke words.

"Pardon me Miss. I just had to tell you my you are such a pretty young lady." he brought those pleasant words to her. "Please let me introduce myself. Jeffries Lagheart."

"Why my name is Martha Manhattan." She replied. "It is very nice to meet you Mr. Lagheart."

"And a pleasure here too." He said as he shook her hand. "With all good pleasures."

"Now please excuse me I must be on my way, Mr. Jeffries Lagheart. And again nice meeting you." She responded as she looked him straight in the eyes.

She then turned as a woman and he'd known then that he had to get to know her. She was as pretty as a summer flower and that was just the beginning of him meeting her. She was out of sight within five seconds. He accidently looked down. There he'd saw a piece of paper on the ground. It had a name, telephone number, and address on it. As he picked it up he read it.

"677 North John St...." said he with a surprise. "I got to see that lady again. Why Miss. Martha Manhattan I just don't know what to say about you..."

It was not long before Martha had checked into a hotel. She was tied and could use a bit to eat. Soon she was about to be sited by the manger. He known that she was a Manhattan. He'd known her because of her father. He was about call her name when she said a few words before he could say anything.

"'A room for one Mr. Swinggy. Here's some extra cash I will be staying awhile." Said Martha Manhattan.

"Why I'd give you the best we have Miss. Manhattan." Said Mr. Swinggy.

"I very much thank you Mr. Swinggy." She said.

She then walked a little and then entered an elevator. Mr. Swinggy then questioned her. He'd wanted to know just how long was she staying. He then walked up towards the elevator and offered to take her luggage. She was just the same old Martha. She'd never give in and all she thought about was the fact that her father had told Joe Holmes to get out of town.

"So tell me Miss. Manhattan how Ions will you be staying?" asked Mr. Swinggy.

"Oh long enough until I can find an apartment Mr. Swinggy." She replied. "Hopefully no longer than two weeks."

"Well you just enjoy your stay. And if there's anything that I can do for you just let me know?" he said as to be helpful.

"Well Sir thank you very much. And I will."

"Well then have a good night Miss. Manhattan." He said.

She then continued and he went back towards his work. He just couldn't believe it. She had given him $5,000.00. That was more than he needed. And plenty extra, since she was only staying two weeks.

"Why that's just like the Manhattans. She just gave me $5,000.00." he numbered to himself.

He was the disquieted. He was then waiting for another customer.

Mr. Swinggy was all but figured it out. What had happened at the Manhattan's? It was not like Ted Manhattan's daughter to just have no place to stay. Had there been a quarrel he wondered. He'd then thought that he'd go and ask just what was going on. He then found himself at Martha's room door.

He became near the door and knocked. Martha then spoke, "Who's there?"

"It's me Martha. It's Mr. Swinggy." Replied Mr. Swinggy.

"Oh Mr. Swinggy?"

"Yes Martha." Said he as he entered the door. "Now

Martha I know that this might not concern me but I'm confused. What'cha doing out this time of night alone."

She then told Mr. Swinggy to come in and close the door. She told him to have a seat. She had a lot of explaining to do. Then she began to tell him that she wanted that most desire that any woman would want. That was that she wanted to take Manhattan and be more powerful than her father Ted Manhattan.

They had met again. Martha was all but innocent of making love now. She was in Jeffries Lagheart's bed and then it was do or die. He'd told her all of his fantasies. She hesitated a bit and then she'd told him all that she had held back from him And all the world. He'd told her all that he wanted out of life now it was her turn.

"So tell me dear what are your most desires in life?" Lagheart asked Martha.

"Oh course a career, education, money, and power." She explained.

"Careers are costly you know?" he stated.

"Oh don't I know?" said Martha.

"And an éducation doesn't come free." Said Jeffries Lagheart.

She got up and took a step towards the window and peeped out across the dark night's sky. There she stood as he watched her figure. She was all but aware of how much he wanted her then. If she'd known would she agree just the same. He then got up with his heroic tall, dark, and handsome muscles in the mist of the night. She'd not heard him creep next to her. Suddenly there was a gentle touch. She'd jerked a little as to be suddenly frightened.

"Oh," said she with fright. "I had no idea that you were there."

"Did I frighten you?" said he as to regret the miler second of it all. Because he'd not want to disappoint her.

"No. no of course not." She replied. "I was just watch the beautiful view across the night's skies."

"My God it is beautiful isn't it?"

"Why yes and I was wondering how could you afford such a place Jeffries? I mean this place must cost you bundles?" said Martha as she looked across the dark room to find his eyes. "You know that's my type of gig. This has always been my dream to own a place like this Jeffries."

"One day you'll reach your dreams Martha." He said as he reach to touch her waist. "But until then just let me hold you in my arms. Would that be alright?"

"You know Jeffries you are very romantic?" said Martha as she gently grabbed his hand and placed it around her waist. "Do you treat all your girls this way?"

"What do you mean?" he asked as he pulsed.

"Why I'm sure that there are hundreds of women who want you?" she replied as to have just a prize even if for one night. "Come on Mr. Lagheart you can tell me?"

"Well Frankly Martha I'm not involved with anyone else right now." Jeffries said as to reassure Martha.

"You don't say," she replied. "Well this night I am in paradise."

She then walked his back slowly to the bed. He was all but in for a treat then. She then loosened the blue gown and his hand touched her breast. It was like no moment ever. They both were in deep lady and man moment of heat. She was in the mood. His lips then touched hers.

It was not long before a beeper went off. It was Martha's. She breath lightly as his hand palmed her thigh. She was more than in the move now. He then thought that he must had been in heaven. She began to mourn. She was calling out his name.

"Jeffries, oh Jeffries, oh honey Jeffries, oh, oh, oh honey it feels good don't stop, don't stop, please never don't stop." said Martha as she began to tell him how much she loved him as a man.

Life was adding up and Jeffries had now made love to Martha. She was good. He was pleased. She had given him the love that he needed. She then got out of the bed placed her hand over her forehead and never felt such a sensation. It was almost as if it was unreal. She then began to think he'd did it. He'd did it good. Were all men like him? Because until a moment ago, she was a virgin. But not anymore, now she was a woman.

She then began to think. What if Ted and Karen Manhattan had found out about that moment. Would they get angry? She hadn't time to worry about that now. She was twenty-nine years old. She had to make it now. She was on her own.

She was once again staring across the dark skies. He then spoke in a soft tone of voice. "How was it?"

"You were wonderful."

"Really?" he asked.

"Yes, I loved it." She said as to be very please with him.

"Well you were good too." Replied Jeffries. "Hey you were terrific."

"I was terrific?" said Martha as to be proud. "You really liked if hun?" "Hey" scout's honor." He once said again. "Martha you are the best. I really truly adore you."

"Well then Jeffries Lagheart you just don't know how good that makes me feel." She said as she stared across the dark skies.

He then step out of the bed. His heroic tall, dark and handsome muscles then threw a shadow on the wall far to the right of the room. She then crept next to him slowly. He wondered if she'd notice that he was staring at her breast. They were unique they were round and seem pleasantly pointy, not to leave out that she was as beautiful as ever with her light Afro American complexion. She was a light colored black American. It went so well with his tall, dark, and handsome partly pose. Although he was thirty-two years old. Martha knew that being only thirty years old it was such a good thing.

He then touched her on the arm and whispered a soft word in her ear. "You know that it was good. But we both have to leave in the morning, so why don't we both get some rest?"

"Yeah," she replied. "I suppose you are right Jeffries."

"Well good let's go to sleep." He said ask her hand caught his.

He then lay down on the bed. She was next to him. She was now at rest.

"Martha honey F d again been meaning to ask you. What is it that you want most out of life?" he questioned as to deeply be concerned.

She then pulsed and in the dark room he'd noticed that the expression on her face was not pleasantly welcomed. She then told him something that she had hid from him and the world a long time. "Well Jeffries if you ask. I want to be more powerful than my father. One day I want to rule Manhattan."

"Martha you can't be serious?" he seemed disappointed. "Why you want'na bring your father down and rule Manhattan? Why would you want'na do that to your father?"

"Because I want power." She insisted.

"Power?" asked Jeffries again. "Don't you love your father that much?"

"No."

"No?" said Jeffries. "I had more faith in you than that Martha."

"Let's just said that it's my greatest desires. And if you love me you would help me?" she managed to look him in the eyes in the dark room.

"Well I do love you." Spoke Jeffries. "What are the plans?"

She went on to tell him the reason she left her Father's house. How she made a bargain with Joe Holmes. She then told parts of her plans.

"You know that Joe Holmes is a drug dealer?" said Jeffries Lagheart. "And he's later to double cross you any time."

"Got plans for that too." Said Martha as she rubbed his chest. She knew that he was wondering what she was going to say next. "And if he does I've got back up."

"So you've really got it all plan out don't you?" he said as to know that this was a very wise lady. "You are still going to need my help still though. I won't let you do this alone."

"I knew- you'd come across Jeffries." Said Martha as she took a deep breath and leaned to his left arm. "Always knew I could count on you."

"Sure you right." He said as to ponder the situation. "Sure you right."

"Well good I'll talk to you more about it later." She said as to feel tied and sleepy.

"Hey I'm here for you." Responded Jeffries.

"Great."

He turned the light switch to dimmer. She was now thinking. She was reassured that she was going to receive victory. What did she have to gain? She had to gain the city of Manhattan. Within thirty days she was going to be ruler of Manhattan. She was going to overrule Ted Manhattan.

"Now Martha you know that your father will let no one

take over Manhattan with out a hell of a fight?" said Jeffries. "You and I are lever to be done with by the end? I mean your father is a powerful man?"

"I know that Father is a powerful man Jeffries. But I've got brain and wit and if anyone knows my father's weakness it's me." She brought those words to him.

"Oh yeah now I'm beginning to feel you. I'm feeling you now." He said as to be a little relieved.

"So Jeffries if you help me take over Manhattan you'd more likely to be Master of Manhattan?" said Martha as to over a life time chance.

"Master of Manhattan?"

"That's right it would be you and I." She said as to promise him.

"Oh what a prize that would be Martha." He exclaimed.

She then politely put her hand over his mouth and said a few words, "get yourself some sleep. Tomorrow's a long day away."

"Hey we were just beginning to plan."

"Shhh, ssss, shhh," she whispered. "Good night."

"Well then good night honey." Said Jeffries.

"Okayyy..."

she then went to sleep and there appeared a dream onto her. She saw a vision. It had something to do with Ted Manhattan. Somehow he became so powerful that the world knew all over the world.

He was known man. In that dream Martha visioned her father talking to her,

"No one will ever out rule me in the city of Manhattan," said Ted Manhattan in her dream. "Not even my dearest do you hear?"

Martha then startled. She was a bit disappoint. It was a dream, but yet it was oh so real. Had her father yet not known even that she wanted to take over Manhattan. She then visioned herself talking back to him.

"You are my father. But it is my greatest desires to rule Manhattan," She pointed out in her dream. "I will rule Manhattan."

"Never." Said Ted Manhattan as he vanished in her dream.

"Oh yeah, one day Manhattan will be all mine, Father." Said insisted.

He was going completely out by then. There were no one who could had done anything more. She then woke out of her dream. She awoke Jeffries also, and he'd not known what was going on.

"Jeffries!"

"What is it?" replied he as he a woke, "My goodness what going on?"

"I had a bad dream Jeffries wake up." She demanded.

"Well Martha it was a dream honey and sometimes dreams frighten us. Hey now lay back down and get some sleep?" he said with concerns.

"Look this was more than an ordinary dream." she said as to have tension on her forehead, "Honey please wake up? We need to talk. You know that I have to go back to my place tomorrow. "Hey we are not married yet."

He was tied and knew that she was serious. Yet, she was Martha and she wanted to talk, He sat up and leaned against the base board of his bed. She had tears pouring from her eyes. She was almost at panic. He had to pull her thru. He had to he was Jeffries he was her man.

"Honey, honey, stop crying it's going to be all right. Wipe your tears. Lay your head on my shoulders and cry." said Jeffries as to want to comfort her.

"It just that it was a bad dream that's all Jeffries." she replied back. "Oh why, why, why, why, Jeffries?"

"Oh now calm down everything's going to be all right." said Jeffries. "Now you know that I am here for you? Don't you Martha?"

"Yes, and I feel safe in your arms." she said with warm words. "You are always there Jeffries when I need you. You truly are."

"That's what I am suppose to do Martha. Just being a gentleman."

She then knew that she had a friend. He was the one that was going to take her to reach her goal. She was going to hand over to her man the jewel of the world Master of Manhattan. She have to leave in a couple of minutes, yet five more days and the weekend would be back again. Then she find her way back to his apartment.

She kissed him on the forehead. He was still asleep, so she did not want to disturb him so she crept out. She was at the bus stop when a little old lady asked her for a quarter. She appeared to Martha as a bag lady.

"Miss." asked the stranger, " have you a quarter?"

"Why yes madam," she replied. "I'd be glad to give you a quarter."

"Why thank you a lot, may the Lord God bless you." Said the strange lady as she walked away. " Good-by."

"Have a nice day. And I'm glad that I could help you." said Martha. "Maybe I could help you again someday."

She thought to herself. What had come over her she was Martha Manhattan. She was going to rule Manhattan how could she rule Manhattan pitting a bag lady? How would that look if the public knew?

Never would she do that again.

There the old lady had taken a couple of steps. It was a plot. She had did it for Ted Manhattan's enemy. She was paid even more than the twenty-five cents. She was paid two grams. Hey when Joe Holmes asked you to move you had to do it or else. But Martha had plans also. She felt that something was up. What and who she had a pretty good idea.

"Holmes you haven't seen the last of me." She shouted as to discovered that there was danger a head. "What you're up to Holmes I got power."

Then she got on the city bus. She had to be on her way to work. Fifteen minutes and she'd be there.

The key to ruling Manhattan was there. Martha had wits. She was squeamish. How could she loose? Then there was a knock at Jeffries Lagheart's door. It was Martha. For some reason she had left work early. She was as if she was pure frightened as a scared lady in doom.

"Jeffries" shouted Martha. "Open the door."

He'd jumped out of bed. "Martha dear, what seems to be the problem?"

"They are after me. You should had been there, there were cars everywhere." replied Martha. "I had to rush quickly and find you."

"Where are we going to go from here?" said Jeffries. "I just let them harm you. Let fly to Italy?"

"Italy?" she quince. "Do you realize what you said? Just what can we accomplish in Italy?"

"A new life."

"If I was you I'd go and jump in a lake." She said angrily. "I thought that you said that we were a team?"

"Jump in a lake? We are a team Martha. I just think that this is the right thing to do right now."

"No damn it, no" responded Martha with a betrayal look. "I want to rule Manhattan, and with or without your help I will."

He went to sat down on the couch. He was puzzled was

this true love or usury. Just a couple of hours ago she was nice, even better she was lovable. Suddenly he'd thought that he should get out of this busy and move on with his life while he was still ahead.

"So you want out Hun?" she had the damned expression on her face. "Go on speak your mind. Do you or do you not?"

"What are you saying? Are you a mind reader of some sort?" he said as wonder as if she was a double crosser. "Look I am a man true to my word. I will help you take over Manhattan."

"Oh you will?"

He then gave her a granting look. " Yes, I will."

"No you won't you fool, get out of my life I'm gone." Said she as the door slammed

"Hey wait, wait, wait, Martha I will." Said as to be serious. "I told you that I would help you didn't I?"

"Yeah, you did Jeffries, but why haven't you done a damn thing now?" said she before he could reply. "You know you are weak, anyone could over take you. By."

There she had made it to there stairways. Things were going as she planned she had him thinking now just as she wanted. He was going to hand her Manhattan. He was puzzled, but she him and she knew him well.

Then Martha said to herself, "It's now October. 6, 2003. 4:00p.m. He'd be wondering I'd went now. But the plans to take over Manhattan is his job not mine. Then the whole world would know just how powerful we are."

Jeffries Lagheart then thought to himself. She was going to leave town. No she couldn't do that. Or could she? He then found himself rushing out the door. Where she she had went he had no idea.

"I'll find Martha if it's the last thing that I do." She was then on the second flight of stairs as he took the elevator. He pressed the first floor button.

She was witty and love was in her heart, and all she had to do was just keep as steady paste.

"Things are on the que," said Martha. "Jeffries go to see Joe Homles now."

"Homles you have not seen the last of me," said Jeffries. "I'm on my way to your house now."

Jeffries hopped into his car and drove off. He didn't know where Martha was. She had made it to the subway. She had a car but the was only person that seen her sheen it, she was the only one, she drove at night.

"Jeffries was at regular speed. He had to find Martha. He had to convince her that he could her her rule Manhattan New York.

She was more than smiling now. There she'd caught up with him and he didn't know that she was driving behind him.

"Smart lady Hun?" Martha thought to herself.

She cruised with a red 2006 Mercedes. Money she had it. Her plans were to never run out. He took a glimpse out of the review mirror. He was two minutes from Holmes place. There he'd reach it.

He got out of his car.

Then she stopped her car. "Hey where are you going?"

"Martha?"

"Yeah," she replied.

"Where did you come from?" he asked.

"Look you have to stop. I mean you don't want to go in there after Joe Holmes." She added. "There are just too many in there."

He thought to himself. She was right. Joe Holmes never lost a fight in his life. How was Jeffries going to over take him? Then he spoke.

"Martha I thought that you had faith in me." He looked her in the eyes. "Just what kind of games are you playing?" "Just get my car. And hurry they are coming."

She started the car she made haste. He thought about his car. There was no turning back. She was not going to be seen by Joe Holmes. Then it all came to him. She had actually planned that. He began to wonder just how wise could this woman get.

"So you knew that I was going to search for you Holmes didn't you?" he asked with a bit of confusion.

"Yeah."

"What else do you know?" said Jeffries

"I know that we are going to take over Manhattan." She said with a smile then cruised.

"Smart lady hun." He thought to himself. "Damned smart."

"So what do you think?" asked Martha. "You like it?"

"What your car?" he said with a smile, and laid back. "It's quite cozy. You know I think I'll take a little nap."

He was all in the groove by then. He was riding in a 2006 Mercedes. Better yet he was riding with his woman, Martha Manhattan. She then turned on her radio. Then she turns it louder, because she thought that the plan had worked. She awoke Jeffries.

"Jeffries, Jeffries honey, you've got to wake up." She said as to tell him bad news. "Your car has been blown to pieces."

"What."

"Yeah, I did it. Part of the plan. Here see." Said Martha as to apologize. " Look I know what know what I am doing ok?"

"Look Martha I loved my car." He had the damned expression on his face. " How am I suppose to travel now?"

" Do you want another one?" replied Martha. " Hey I asked you a question."

"Martha you do have to buy me a new car, ok?" she looked him in the eyes the way he guided hers. Then he said a few more words. " Hey I'll get me another one ok?"

Then she suddenly told him to get out, "Hey you've got to hurry get out."

"Hey, why are you putting me out?" he demanded an explanation. " You can't just leave me in the middle of town."

"Look we got to make them think that you are dead."

"What?" he shattered.

"Just get back in, hurry," she said as to be very nervous. "Hurry don't say another word just hurry."

"What's this all about?"

"Didn't you see that boom?" she asked. "Damn it Jeffries, that's the first thing that my Father Ted Manhattan taught me to live here in Manhattan."

Then she drove off. It was as if Jeffries was in a dais. Martha was scheming. She was going have to come up with an explanation if she wanted to see Jeffries tomorrow. Then she had a similar expression on her face.

"So you're wondering what I'm doing aren't you?" said she as she hid her fears. "Hey it's just like I said I want to rule Manhattan, and I'll do anything for it Jeffries."

She then had a tear fall from her eye, not the tear of sadness, but the tear of madness. She told him to meet her at his apartment if the deal was still on.

"Here get out and meet me the in thirty minute if the deal is still on." She added as if she really trusted and needed his help.

He got out and went to the subway. He then began to wonder. Was he the target? After all, he met her later one night, with her luggage and a purse, she had. He was in a rush. Thirty minute to get to his apartment was a boom rush. It took God to let him get there. It was not long before he bumped into another lady. He looked her in the eyes and went his way.

"Excuse me Miss., I had no intention bumping into you." He said as to freeze. " You eyes seem familiar, please excuse me."

He had taken about fifteen steps. Then it crossed his mind. She looked Exactly like Martha Manhattan. Something was going on. He had questions, and Martha was going to answer them or else. Then there was a gentleman on the subway. He gave Jeffries something that he said was somewhat a bit of knowledge.

"Take it from me son you don't want to get involve with her." Said the stranger as he walked away. " Now just a bit of knowledge."

Then Jeffries thought to himself, he had questions. " Hey, wait who are you and why did you say that?" He was confused.

Then the subway pulled off.

He decided to call Martha. He was beginning to get angry. She had damned to answer his questions.

Martha answered her cellar phone. "Wow! That was quick. Are you home Jeffries?"

"No Martha and I've got questions when we get there." He was tied and wanted a bit of rest. But how could he rest when he fell in love with a woman who had a hell around him. "Now I still love you but I just really got to know, what's going on?"

"Ok, when I get thee we can talk."

"Well that's all I ask." He shut his phone down. Then said to an old lady sitting across from him. "Just had a bad day that's all."

"I know what you mean son." She replied. "I get them sometimes too."

"Boy, glad I'm not by my self?"

"You're not." She added. " Believe me son you're not."

"Well thank you for your comforting words" then he sat back in his seat.

"Son God is Good." Said she. "and you can't take away from it or add to it." Then the subway stopped. She got off and said, "Have a nice night son."

"Thank you. And you too."

He had never seen that old lady again.

But he was happy.

Martha had made it to Jeffries house. He had just crept the sidewalk next to her car. She was disappointed in a way, because he didn't stop walking. He passed the car. She the found herself jumping out of her car. She got angry.

"Hey Jeffries what's this? You just pass me like that?" she stared him in the eyes. "I thought you were better than that. I'm out of here."

"No we need to talk."

"Talk?" she asked as to damn him.

"Yeah, Martha there is something that you are not telling me." He decided to sit on the front porch. "Come and sit with me."

"No."

"Oh come on Martha." He said as he remembered the first night they spent together. "You are going to be the same old Martha aren't you?"

"Don't try to charm me Jeffries. I know better. You are trying to back down now." She straight forward marched. "But if you do I'll find someone else."

"Martha," asked Jeffries. "How much do you hate your father?"

"I don't hate him I just love him to deaf." She said with a powerful tongue.

Jeffries was a smart guy. Martha wanted it her way. Had her father done any harm to her when she was young? Something was up. She sat beside him and she told him to go on and talk.

"Talk." Said Martha. "I'll listening. What's up?"

"That's what I want you to tell me." Said Jeffries Lagheart with a bit of fright. "I thing have been going on that I don't know about. I mean to tell you the truth Martha I don't want to upset your father. He'd later to hang me."

"Are you saying that you don't trust me?" Said she as he turned his eyes away. "Oh God Jeffries."

" No, I didn't say that." Replied Jeffries. " Ted Manhattan is a man Martha and a great one."

"So you want out I'm gone."

"Hey wait a minute." He stopped her. "You think that I let you down?

"Yeah, Jeffries that white man Joe Holmes is trying to take over Manhattan and you're so weak, such a weak man that you won't help a sister out." She got angrier. "So if you want out the reward go you free you're out."

"It just that you don't understand right now." He added.

She walked out and had the look on her face as to say you fail me. Her pose began to close to him now. She was serious. She was Martha Manhattan and the day was coming that Manhattan was going to be hers. It was not long before she brought out a telephone. The plan was still was becoming a master minded woman.

"Hello Father?" said a voice not to be heard in weeks. "This is Martha."

"Martha?"

"Yes, Father I'm just calling to let you know that I'm

doing fine." She said as to be in a rush. "You take care now, got' a go."

"But Martha..." before he could say another word she had hung up. "You have not given me time to talk."

She got into her car. She turned on her radio. Something was up. Joe Holmes had put out a reward for anyone who could tell him who had blown up that car that was in front of his mansion. Martha giggled. He'd not known that she had better plans than that to run him out of Manhattan New York.

"Karen?" said Ted Manhattan. "Looks like Martha's up to something. And damn it I can't figure it out."

"What?" she replied. " How did you know Ted?"

"She just told me."

Karen, Martha's Mother began to get very upset. The thought of her daughter out on a scheme, made her wonder what kind of daughter did she raise, whole entire life would had dreamed that Martha would had turn out like this."

"Karen?" said Ted. "The "What are we going to do Ted?" responded Karen. "I'd never in my re's something that you are over looking. Martha is one of us, she a Manhattan."

"I know but Ted, she out there all alone."

"Karen trust me she can and will take care of herself, and what ever she wants to conquer, she will do just that." Said Ted Manhattan with a smile. "I have just that much faith in her."

"Well what ever you say Ted Manhattan." The moment seemed odd to her but then she said, "just don't regret what you're saying. Now you just and remember that."

"I will Karen, we have raised a fine daughter. Very well trained to defend herself and Manhattan" said Ted with not a bit of regrets.

Karen then walked into the room and asked. "Did she say anywhere she could be reached?"

"No Karen now quit worrying, ok?" he was sincere.

"How can I Ted?" she said with an angry voice. "You sound as if that's not my daughter. Look Ted nothing better not happen to our daughter or you are the blame and I mean that. Now that's final."

Karen walked out into the kitchen as see drew her eyes from his. She remembered the first time that they move into the house. Martha was only twelve years old. She loved watching her Mother bake cookies. Now she was all grown up, and left home and Karen had no idea where she was, could Ted had been right was this one of Joe Holmes plans, to get their daughter out of there house for some reason. She thought when they'd caught up with Holmes he'd better have a good explanation.

"I hear you Karen." He sighed. "Now you have got to realize, this bothers me just as much as it bothers you."

"Oh if you say so Ted" she poked him in the chest. "Then tell me Ted why in two weeks you haven't heard from your own daughter?"

Ted then had hard feelings. The room began to feel cool to him. She was out there and he had the slightest clue of where she could be. Something held Ted back from walking out that door to find Martha, what was it?

"It's just that I've got to give it time." Said Ted as to mean business.

"Time?" she demanded an explanation.

He walked out the kitchen. His red color black complexion began to fail him as a strong man. He was puzzled. He had never felt like that before. What was he to do? His wife began to lose faith in him. She wanted him to walk out that door. He couldn't Martha would make it on her own.

Martha had to find a strategy to keep her Father from knowing exactly was going on. She known that if he'd known that she was double crossing him with a man to over rule Manhattan, although she was his daughter, he'd take or run her out of the city of Manhattan New York. She was on her way to her house, when someone flagged her down. It looked liked Jeffries, he was walking in the rain. She stopped her 2006 Mercedes.

"Jeffries, is that you?" she said as she remembered when she told him that she blow his new car up. " Honey, you need to get in the car."

"Martha?" replied Jeffries. " I was just on my way to your house."

He got in the car. He was a bit hesitant, but she told him that she knew that he was soaked wet, but it was ok.

"So you really mean it's ok to get in soaked wet?" Responded Jeffries as he felt compassion.

"Hey girl scout honor." She assured him.

He slid back and tried to get comfortable. The way was strange to him. Way did he love this woman so much? Was it because from the very first night that he'd laid eyes on her he'd fell in love. He loved her and it was plain to him. He'd do anything to defend her.

She then said, "So you were on your way to my house?" she said as to wonder just where was he headed. "Look Jeffries is there something that you are not telling me?"

"Well yes Martha, it's just that you are the only one who seems to know the plans of what's going on, why not help me out here?"

"Ok what do you want to know?"

"Of coarse number one is, am I in danger?" he said with a great shiver.

"First of all do you really trust me?" she asked as to

know what was really on his heart. "Because if you did you would've known that I will protect you by now."

"I'm just confused, that's all, and I need to know now." Said he as he'd never experienced nothing like it before.

"Well then let me tell you. You are in no danger Jeffries, I reassure you." Said Martha as she cruised down the streets. With her red 2006 Mercedes.

"Thank you God. Thank you Lord,"

She knew that she'd comforted him. It was just part of her plan, and everything was running on schedule. In 7 day Martha Manhattan was going to be Master of Manhattan. She began to wonder did Jeffries really trust in her? She'd thought that she told him the truth. Could it had been that Jeffries was as hard hearted as her Father Ted Manhattan?

There they'd reached his apartment. He was sleeping. She woke him up. Here were two that loved each other and nothing would break them apart.

"Jeffries?"

"Yes, Martha?" said Jeffries as their eyes met in the misty night. "Are we there?"

"Yes, we are at your house." Replied Martha.

"My crib?" said he as he glanced at the stars.

She told him that she would help him get out of the car. Because she didn't want anything to happen to him. They had made it into hi apartment. She was thrilled. Every time that she when there she remembered the first time he made love to her.

"Thank you dear for helping me into my apartment." Said Jeffries with a sincere heart. "I really mean that."

"You're welcomed dear," said Martha with a smile.

He sat on the couch. She poured him a glass of wine. The moment was like old times. The skies were beautiful. The city of New York had more than opportunity to offer a killer of an ink pen, merely a writer trying to make it in the writing business. His name was Jeffries Lagheart.

"Jeffries," said Martha as she laid next to him. "Are you comfortable honey?"

"Martha with you by my side, I'm always comfortable." Replied Jeffries.

"Oh yeah, then tell me why'd you say that?"

"Well the plain out true is that I love you Martha." He said with a sincere heart, as their eye met he kissed her on the cheek.

There the wind gentle blew the curtain. He'd have to do one thing and that was that he'd have to ask Martha again what does so much power mean to her? She was about to take her very Father out. That he could not understand.

"Kindly tell me what does power means to you?" said Jeffries as to not want to anger her. "Now you can take your time I'm not in no rush."

"Just what's your point?"

"Think Martha?" replied Jeffries. "If you took over Manhattan New York, who would take over you?"

"Look Jeffries that'll never happen." Said Martha as she beamed him in the eyes. " I am too smart for that, Jeffries."

" Martha I know that you are smart, but I love you and want nothing to happen to you." He replied. "So still as I know you, you are going on with your plans. Aren't you?"

He slid back with his back on the bed rail. She was bitter. Hadn't he known the Manhattans by now? Although she loved him should she show his a lesson or two? She had plans but she also knew that he could doubt her somewhere down the line.

It was not long before Martha had dimmed the bedroom lights. She was in the mood. He was too. He unbuttoned her red dress. Kiss her. She laid on the bed. His pose was black tall, with her red light color Afro American complexion which matched her Mother and Father's.

"I have to do what I have to do Jeffries," said Martha as his hand met her thigh. "But of course you do under me don't you Jeffries?"

"Honey, why of coarse, of coarse." Responded Jeffries as to reassure her.

"Then good," she said as they made love. "She started to call his name, Jeffries, Jeffries, Jeffries, don't stop don't stop."

"Honey, believe me I won't"

There Martha cellar phone had rung. It was her Mother. There was something bad going on at the house. Ted told Martha that she needed to get over there soon. She needed to stay awhile with her Mother Karen. Before Ted hung up her told Martha that he'd heard some pretty bad news going on around town about her. Yet, he didn't say what it was, because he still loved his daughter. But, no one double cross him.

"Father, what are you talking about?" she said as ever be frighten from her father before. "Listen do you think that I'm hiding something from you?"

"Yes, Martha and I think you know what it is?" he said as to mean that she make haste to get over there. "Now hurry and get over here don't keep Karen and I waiting, ok?"

"Ok, Father." Said she as just to wonder as what he was talking about.

She stared into the dark skies of Jeffries apartment. What was going on? Had Ted figured it out? Everyone knew that he was a smart man. No that couldn't have happened. The plan that she'd drew up for five years was failing now. No.

Jeffries looked at the expression that was on Martha's

face. He began to ask questions. She hesitated. But, then she broke out into tear and cried. "Oh, Jeffries, why, why, why?"

He felt her weary. He had to figure out a way to help her. Although he feared her Father Ted Manhattan, he had to make her wish come true, and that was that she was going to become Master of Manhattan. Jeffries Lagheart, a young man from the south, hadn't come to the city of Manhattan to back down off a situation like this, for this was his opportunity.

"So Martha hon, who was that on the phone?" he said with a great concern. " I mean you know me by now. You can talk to me about anything. Ok?"

"No Jeffries I can't tell you." Said her as to be frightened. "Because if I did you and I both later be done for."

"Listen to me Martha?" replied he. "Who ever that was they can't hurt you. I got your back ok?"

"No. I will not tell you. Sorry I've got to go." Martha kissed him on the cheeks then she head out the doors. " But I promise you that I'll get back in contact with you."

"Hey wait a minute." He tried to stop her. "Can't you at least tell me who it was?"

"No." sadly she walked out the door. "I must go it is very necessary."

"Well then do like you said, please come back?" he said with feelings.

"Trust me Jeffries I will be back. Because we are down like That." She replied. "I know that you've got my back."

Jeffries Lagheart then brought a smile to his face. Even if he'd never seen her again he'd always remember her words. She never lied to him, not that he'd known. She saw that look on his face. It was like 'Baby are you really coming back?'

She closed the door. He then got out of bed. He couldn't

let her go by herself. She was his woman. He had to help her out. She then got into her car, and drove off.

He then got to the corner near his apartment, "Martha honey wait. I am here to help you. Don't just leave with out me."

It was too late. She was nowhere in sight.

She had brought tears to her eyes. She had seen times when her Father really roughed up people for bugging his city. She didn't want that to happen to her. She began to lament.

It was not long before her phone rung. "Hello, Martha speaking?"

"Martha honey I can't let you go there alone." Said Jeffries. "I just can't honey."

"Jeffries this is something that I must do alone."

Sadly Jeffries wanted to say why. But, he'd already knew the answer. She was Martha Manhattan and she was a thirty years old light skinned American and she was never going to change.

He headed back to his apartment. Surly he'd get no rest that night. Martha then brought out her cellar phone. Jeffries didn't know it but things were going as she'd planed. Two more weeks and four days she was going to rule Manhattan.

"Hello, Father, is that you?" asked Martha.

"Yes, this is I Martha, where are you?" he demand. "And please tell your Mother and I where are we getting this bad news when you get over here."

"Ok, Father, be right over."

Although Martha was hard hearted and wanted to rule Manhattan. She still respected her Mother, Karan Manhattan, her first love. Ted was seemly mad. Martha knew it. But, no one could stop her now not even Joe Homles. She had no idea what to expect when she'd gotten there. Would she even be banded and carried out of the city like other men that tried to double cross her Father? No? But by chance?

"I knew just what to tell Mother when I get there." She said to herself. I never lied to her before but I am out of reasons.

Jeffries Lagheart knew that he had to find Martha. She was his lady. He got out of bed. He put his clothes on and headed for the door. There could by no chance could Martha get hurt. She was his first love, although he didn't understand all of her plans. He began to reason with himself.

"Martha is headed towards her Father and Mother." He said with fear to himself. "Could Ted had known her plans?"

He had made it to the subway. The train was there. He'd have to ride about eight minutes.

It was not long before his cellar phone had rung. "Hello, this Jeffries Legheart. Whom may I ask is speaking?"

"Jeffries?" said a gentle voice.

"Yes," he replied. " Martha?"

"Look honey, I'm sorry that I had to leave right away." She said as to feel that she'd let him down. "I should had told you where I was going."

"Martha there is nothing that you can do that I don't understand." Responded Jeffries Lagheart. "So hey where are you headed?"

"Honey as much as I would like to I can't tell..." a tear fell from her eye as she hung up the cellar phone.

"But honey please I lov..." she'd hung up before he could say anything.

She began to cruise the streets with her 2006 red Mercedes. She cut her radio on, just at that instant she'd seen Joe Holmes car pass by. It made her mad to think that he thought that he could take over Manhattan New York.

There was no way that she was going to let that happen. She was too smart and witty.

"Well that's just like old Martha," said Jeffries Lagheart to himself. "A young lady that does it by herself, and never gives up."

Martha had arrived at her Father's apartment. There her Mother was to greet her at the door. She knew that her Father meant business and wanted to talk to her.

"Martha?"

"Yes, Mother?" said Martha. "It is I."

"Well come in." replied her Mother. "Oh I'm so glad to see you."

"Oh Mother and I'm glad to see you too." Said Martha.

"Well we'd been lonely every since you left Martha." She sadly said. "Hon why don't you come back home?"

"Just can't Mother, I'm a Manhattan and I must make it on my own." Said Martha with a bit of pride. "Right now Mother I must make it on my own sorry."

There was still in the air. Martha wanted to see just what did her Father want to see her for. He walk out of her parents bedrooms and began to speak.

"Well congratulations on making it on your own for two weeks." Said Ted Manhattan her Father with pride. And by the way Martha my dear daughter happy, happy birthday."

Tears began to pour down her eyes. She was almost at faint. She then told her Father and Mother that she could not stay she had to leave.

"Father I really appreciate this but however I can not accept this birthday party." Said Martha as she walked out the door. " Good-by I must go."

She then walked out the door, her Mother ran to the door and said, "Martha dear we love you come back."

"Sorry Mother."

"No," said Ted Manhattan. "I'm the one that's sorry, I should've known better than to try."

"Maybe Father."

It hurt Karen Manhattan, Martha's Mother. She began to think that she was losing her daughter. What had become of her? Martha was up to something, could Ted Manhattan had known and tried to talk her out of it.

Ted Manhattan walked into their bedroom. Karen followed. She loved her husband. He reminded him of his father. Yeah, James Manhattan, Ted Manhattan's Father was a strong man, he was able to get himself out of every situation.

"Ted." Said a questioning voice. "Are you alright?"

"Well Karen, I tried my best." Responded Ted. " And you know I'm never giving up on my daughter."

Then Karen said a few words, "Now you just wait one minute here, I will not have you saying your daughter, Ted Manhattan, she our daughter. Ok?"

"Yes, ok Karen."

He then remembered how beautiful she was the first day that he met her. It was in North Carolina in a little town called Elizabeth City. She was the finest woman in town. Money couldn't buy her. A man had to have wisdom.

"Karen darling come to me." Said he as to feel love. " I need one of your sweet kisses."

"Oh, Ted you big man you."

"I'm your Husband." He replied with a smile.

"Don't I know," they kissed.

He then laid her on the bed.

They had slept together the night passed. Karen was the only woman that Ted Manhattan wanted. She was kind and loving. He love that in her. One day somehow her was going to prove that to her.

"So you really think that she's going to make it on her own, do you not," said Karen as to peep and see the rising sun. "I never doubt you before so I have no reason to doubt you now Ted Manhattan." She Karen as she marched into the bathroom.

"Thank you dear." Said Ted. "I love you. And I really mean that."

It was not long before there were sirens going off. Martha wondered just what was going on. Jeffries was curious too, as Martha cruised down the streets with her 2006 Mecedez. She stopped parked the car. The rumor had it that Joe Holmes had been shot. It struck the whole city of New York. Nobody shoots Joes Holmes. Holmes a white gentleman about the age of thirty-five, red hair, and stand six-foot tall, slim, would get his vengeance. He wouldn't die without it.

"Jeffries?"

"I heard Martha." Said Jeffries. "Who could got'ten that close to him to pull a rig like that? Who would had been so witty?"

"I have the one just in mind," said Martha as she felt a bit of fright. "Someone who just does not play around."

"But who Martha?"

Martha then slowed down and began to think. Could her guess had been right? Would the person that she was thinking of actually shoot a person? No? But by chance?

"Martha honey do we need to talk." Replied Jeffries Lagheart. " Because I think that there is something that you are just not telling me? Ok?"

"You know Jeffries I'm beginning to thing that you are beginning to doubt me again." Exclaimed as to be disappointed. "You should know me better by now."

As she said that she said open my car pocket Jeffries, out of the mist of nowhere. He wondered just what was going on. Why did that facial expression on her face change suddenly? "Open the damn car pocket Jeffries."

"What?" scared words came out of his mouth. "Just what's going on Martha?"

"What's in the car pocket?" said Martha as she open it herself, and brought out a white handkerchief with something wrapped in it. "That's who shoot Joe Holmes."

"What? You mean you..."

"Exactly." Said Martha as she put the weapon back in the car pocket. " He damn well deserved it."

"But, Martha I knew that you had plans, but you shot Joe Holmes?" he couldn't believe his ears as to double check himself. " But shooting Joe Holmes is unreal."

"Who did I tell you that I wanted to become Master of Manhattan? Even to take over my very Father Jeffries Lagheart?" she demand his response.

"Why you said you and I Martha. Have your plans changed?? Said her as wondering could he trust her. " Are we still in this game together?"

"What do you think?"

"I say yeah." He said as to reassure her.

"Then let's finish Joe Holmes off?" replied Martha.

"Martha?"

"What is it Jeffries?" a strong look was in her eyes.

"That's Joe Holmes. One of the biggest men in Manhattan New York." Said Lagheart with a bit of fright.

"And I'm Martha Manhattan."

"And your man Jeffries Lagheart, so let's do this." Said he.

"Let's go." She kissed him and beamed down the road.

They were beaming down the road. Martha knew that she have accomplish this one. She had to it was part of her marvelous plans, and Jeffries Legheart her man was going to help her carry it out. Then he spoke.

"Do you still love me baby?" said Jeffries as to know tha he had a real woman. "Martha hon, can you hear me? What's the next game plan?"

"Would you like something to drink?" asked Martha.

"Sure thing where from?"

KELLEY'S

"That'll be a bet." replied Jeffries.

She then turned in the driveway. They entered the bar. He had never been there before. She then looked around. "Hey, nice place hun?"

"Yeah I'd say."

"Well good, the regular for the both of us Kelly." said Martha as to have pull.

"Sure Ms. Manhattan."

"Martha Kelly this is just a friend you can call me Martha." replied Martha.

"Sure thing, Ms. I mean Martha." responded Kelly.

He put his hand over on hers.

What would Ted do if he'd seen his daughter like this wondered Kelly. He then went to take care of the order, "Oh well."

There they drunk one, and out the door. She then told Jeffries that she meet him at her place. In an half an hour. He said that she'd better not be late. For Martha never broke a promise to him. He then got out and walk four blocks. 'Damn it what was she up to?' But hey she was Martha she was his girl.

He began to hear foot steps. The faster he began to walk the were the footsteps catching up to him. He decided to stop. There the footsteps had stopped. He started back walking the footsteps then started back up. At that moment Jeffries was tied, and he wanted no trouble. He decided to stop again.

"Ok who are you?"

"You don't know?" replied the low strange voice. "Think if you will Mr. Legheart?"

"Oh come on it's late out here."

He began to think back. He couldn' think of no one. Give me a hint he requested.

"You know you just might could remember more if you'd stopped smoking them darn cirgerttes."

Then he paulsed. Who was she telling to stop smoking his cigerttes? He began to get angry.

Then the stranger said, "Before you get angry. I don't play games."

"And whom may I ask are you?" asked Jeffries Lagheart. "I mean your voice sounds as a stranger Madam."

"Do you remember the old lady that you saw on the subway just the other night?" replied the voice. "Talk now or else you're wasting my time."

"The other night, why I spoke to hundreds of old women the other night, Madam." said Jeffries Lagrheart with a curious voice. "Why I'd bet that you could say just the same, now couldn't you?"

"Hold it buster don't be such a wise guy. Now I know what you are up to. Now I want in or else..."

"Or else what?" fearful expressions appeared on Jeffries face.

"Or else I'd just have to let Ted Manhattan know." she said as she walked away.

Then Jeffries thought, "How do you know that he does not already know?"

"Because he doesn't." she reassured him. "Just bare that in mind."

As she walked away Jeffries began to get nervous. "Hey what's your name, how can I contact you?"

"I'll get back wit you." said the strange voice. "Now you just think about what I said."

He didn't know what to think. How could he explain that to Martha. A stranger

It was not long before Jeffries cellar phone had wrong. It was Martha she was excited. She had great news and it made her feel grand. He was trying to tell her that he had bad news and she was not going to like it. She would just would not shut up. He had to stop her from talking.

"Martha honey I need to talk to you." said Jeffries with patients. "Martha there is a bit of bad news."

"Bad news?.."

"Yes. That's what I've been trying to tell you. An old lady had been on my trrail for sometime now and damn well knew all about there set up... She pulled out a .38 caliber and mentioned indeed that she wanted a piece of Manhattan New York." He went on with the conversation. "Honey she didn't mention her name, but said that she'd get back in contact with me and told me to think about it."

"Jeffries damn Jeffries why didn't you get her name?" said Martha as to hide something. "Damn that could had been her."

"What?" surpraised, "Who... did you know her Martha?"

He began to think. He'd be in big trouble if he kept on messing with this woman. Was she leading him down the wrong track? He 'd heard about the Manhattans long ago. That's why he'd came to New York. Sure New Yorker's were witty but he had to put it to the task. He'd told his Mother at five old that he was going to see

If New York was New York. He told that one day he was going to become a writer and try the most powerful person in New York. He said he was going. His Mother told him that he was not going alone. "Now do you know who the strange voice of an old lady was with the .38 caliber?" His very own Mother his back down Mrs. Lisa N. Lagheart from North Carolina, had arrive own time to protect her son.

"No I do not know who that stranger was," Martha even became a bit confused herself. "Darn it."

"But Martha I think that there is something that you are not just telling me." responded Jeffries as to feel betrayed. "Now I thought that we were a team, right?"

"Yes, Jeffries , we are a team but I...never seen the lady... hold it wait a minute.

I seen her once before," she said thinking back.

"Where?" Jeffries wanted to know instantly. "Where?"

"At the subway when I followed you the other night." said Martha. "I stopped and parted the car as soon as you got out of the car."

"What?" he needed an answer, "Martha, this is not beginning to sound right just what's going on here?"

She looked him in the eyes straight forward, and said, "I got the plan remember Jeffries?" As she walk away. Things were on time.

Jeffries began to think. Had she tricked him? Sure they met on that wonderful night, but there was a time to quit. There was a time to give up. He was at that age he was in a city that they call Manhattan New York. Sure he'd given it a fight but where was God? Did he exist? It was like poison to his tongue. Yet, if they'd take his life that would satify him.

At the moment he was dying slowly. Where was Mother? She hadn't fooled Jeffries. She and her daughter loved their lovers more than they'd loved Jeffries. Yet, after they'd slowly killed him, they would bring them to odd cities and slowly tarment the hell out of them slow. He'd realized that once you'd died you never come back. But, what was death to him. To him death was priceless, one couldn't love such a thing more than he.

"Martha," he said. "Come back here"

"No I've got some place to be." she said as she picked up her pace. "Later, Jeffries I'll get back with you."

"If you leave I'm going back to North Carolina." he meant business. "Mean it Martha. You then would never become Master of Manhattan."

She felt betrayed all that she'd done for him. She gave it a thought to turn around, but then she thought to herself. She was Martha Manhattan. "Then suit yourself leave I'll do it myself."

"I will good-by." said Jeffries as to take control. "I will."

Then she turned around. "You know what Jeffries?"

He answered. "What?"

"You are scared."

"Of what?" replied as to wait for a definite answer. "Of what?"

"Of life."

"Life?" he took a watchful look.

"Yes life." said Martha. "You shouldn't be eating everything because Sherimanatan and Michael Carlie told you to eat years ago. You knew that these people poison you and your grandfather. All I'm saying is stop eating people's food they will try to poison you take your life. Once you are gone God will tend to them but not before Jeffries. Pull your on weight. Even if you have to go to College and get many degrees and eat nothing but crackers there will come a G day for you."

"I will take your advice learn and for now on I will take nobody advice but yours', books, counselor. And not even my sister's, nor my Mother's, nor my Aunts, nor my Uncles, nor my Bro's, nor his Daddy's." said Jeffries. " I'm down with you and that's forever, ok, agreed upon?"

"Yes, agreed upon."

"Thank you." they shook hands.

Martha then told Jeffries that she'd meet him at his apartment in about an hour. She told him that if that stranger with the strange voice came back, get her name and let her know who she was. They both departed from the scene after a kiss on the cheeks. Martha at that point knew what she had to do. Within fifteen minutes no matter how frightful she was, she'd have to meet Joe Holmes down the alley, as she told him. She'd then let him know who shot him in the right arm. She knew he'd kill. But, Martha's plans never failed her.

She had parked her car. She looked into her car pocket. There was no gun, there was no red handkerchief. She began to get nervous. Some one was snooping, and she thought that she knew just who it was, "Joe Holmes."

She gave it thought to turn back around. She couldn't face Joe Holmes with out protection. Yeah, she'd admit now that she was Martha Manhattan, but that was Joe Holmes that she was dealing with.

There was a strange voice like none she'd ever heard. It was Joe Holmes. "Hello Martha."

"Ms. Manhattan if you please?"

"Believe me I dearly please." he replied as to feel a bit of pain.

"Mr. Holmes you don't quite sound like yourself." said Martha. "Why? Oh never mind I realize now you've been shot. Just don't know about that."

"Let's get on with business, tell me who shot at my right arm as if they'd tried to kill me?" asked Joe Holmes. "Now you said it was free but I'm willing to pay you Martha."

"Ms. Manhattan if you please?"

"Oh come on Martha this is Holmes that you are talking to." replied Joe Holmes. "I don't answer to no one."

"You want to know don't you?" exclaimed Martha. "Just can't get over it can you?"

"Hell no I can't."

"Jeffries Lagheart." said Martha as she walked quickly away, and drove off. "Jeffries Lagheart was the one that shot. Good-by."

Then Holmes found himself saying, "Why that dirty scum." He then got on the phone. "Baldman, I need you to listen and to listen good."

"What's up Joe?" asked Baldman, "Is there trouble?"

"Yeah, I just found out who shot at me." replied Joe Holmes. "And I need him killed now, ok?"

"Who is he?"

"Jeffries Lagheart, Martha Manhattan's old man." said Joe Holmes with rushing words. "Wipe him out…"

"Well Joe as you know I've got to get paid so me and the grew will wipe him out." replied Baldman, "Is there anybody else?"

"Yeah while you're at it take care of his old lady too." said Joe Holmes as to have no compassion. "She's probably the only eilliby."

"By the way Joe what's the cost?" asked Baldman. "He's bound told to be witty I need to know what'cha paying?"

"Baldman, Baldman."

"Ok, ok, ok, just a little joking there." replied Baldman.

"Yeah, I hear you." said Holmes as if he didn't want time wasted. "Then go and get the job done."

"We on our way."

Joe Holmes then hung his phone up. He had doubt about the situation . There were time that Baldman accomplished great acheivements that Joe sent him on, but something was odd about this situation. Could Baldman been heading for a target? What was it that frightened Joe this time?

"Somehow I don't believe he's coming back." bitter words mummbered Joe Holmes, as he got into his car a 2007 Mazaradee, blue, two doors and a five speed.

"Well in case he does I'll pay him good."

Then there was a still in the alley alone. Debris began to blow.

Martha had to reach Jeffries to let him know what she had did. She had lied on Jeffries. But that was part of the plan. It was to lure all of Joe Holmes men to Jeffries Lagheart's place. Then there was going to be a great show down. She decided to get on her cellar phone and call Jeffries.

The phone rung about five times. But there was no answer. Jeffries would had usually answered by then. Martha began to get worried, and so she dailed again. He still didn't pick up. What could had been the problem?

"Darn it," said Martha as to be a bit confused. "I should had known he's not going to answer his cellar phone, well ok I'll just have to handle this myself."

Martha had totally forgotten that she'd told Joe Holmes that Jeffries was the one that shot him, of course she did at first she was going to tell the truth, but she became weak stumbled and saw that there were about fifteen of Joe Holmes' men there with guns. What was she to do?

"Well let me try again." Martha said as she pulled out her cellar phone.

"Hello?" said a slight gentleman like voice. "This is Jeffries Lagheart?"

"Jeffries?"

"Yes, this is Jeffries Lagheart."

"Jeffries honey you need to get out of your apartment and I mean soon. I can't fully explain it right now, but there's about to be a show down, ok babe?" pulse.

"Martha honey what in the heck is going on?" asked Jeffries, "I mean out of nowhere you tell me to leave town."

"Jeffries, just get out of your apartment honey, meet me at my place in about a half of an hour." she replied as to have no time to waste. "Look just do it."

"Ok, Martha, and we have got to do some serious talking when we meet at your place Martha." he exclaimed. "And I mean this."

"Believe me Jeffries I know that we have got to do serious talking, but you just don't know how serious it is, ok?" she mummbered to herself.

"Hey be there in a half an hour." he meant business.

"I will, Jeffries darlin' I will." she said as to humble herself.

She hung her phone up. She began to wonder was this a time to fear, hey sure she was Martha Manhattan, but things where beginning to move quickly. Would she be the one to end up in a sham? Could not only Ted Manhattan, her Father, herself, Joe Holmes, could there had been a separate party trying to take over also?

"Darn it where are my keys" said Jeffries to himself.

"Well." said Martha to herself, "I've only got four more days to take over Manhattan New York. Then Jeffries and I will be known as the greatest rulers that ever lived"

He the started his new car, "Martha, things are beginning to get complicated."

Martha was going about the normal speed limit. She would hang in there. Of course she had a point to prove and a goal to reach. But sooner or later everyone was going to know how witty she was, the Master of Manhattan, Martha Manhattan. Jeffries began to wonder. Just what was Martha's plans. She had never really given him a view of the blue print. Jeffries decided to give Martha a phone call.

"Hello, this is Martha speaking. How may I help you?" said Martha as not have a clue of who it was.

"Jeffries Martha. Why are you not here yet?" said Jeffries as to be a bit angry.

"Honey, there's been a bit delay. You see I told Joe Holmes that you shot him." said Martha as to hide a bit of fear.

"What?"

"Yeah." replied Martha. "Are you mad."

"Martha no." responded Jeffries. "Because I know that you have a plan. And your plans Martha always work."

"Well good. I'll be right over." she kissed thru the phone.

"Well hurry because it's about to rain."

He then unlocked Martha's door, and went inside. He peeked to see was there a strange woman following him as he cut out the lights. Then he called someone.

"Hello, this Janu Ed Valezquez, how may I help you?" said a voice that many never knew that had recently just gotten in Manhattan New York. It was Jeffries Lagheart's brother. "Again speak."

"Hello bro' did you take care of the dirty works?"asked Jeffries. "Because I'm really to take Martha back home."

"I did Bro'."

"What did you do to make me becomed Master of Manhattan?" replied Jeffries. "Because I need to know."

"I did everything that Martha Manhattan's plans from day one told me to do." then Janu Ed Valezquez hung his phone up. "That was send Joe Holmes on a wild goose chase he went some Island for gold where he'd end up who know

Martha somehow had gotten the news that there was a new man in town. Who he was she had no idea. But, she had means to find out. She decided to call Jeffries. She'd known that that was part of his job. He then picked up his phone.

"Hello, Jeffries Lagheart speaking." said Jeffries as to walk out of his house. "Whom may I ask is speaking?"

"Hello it's me Jeffries, Martha." she said as lo be closer to her goal with her man. "There's this stranger that I hear that's in town. By thae name Janu Ed Valezquez do you know of him?"

"Of course Martha that's my bro..." then Jeffries was hit by a briefcase and he fell to the grouud.

Then there was an unfamiliar voice that spoke. "So you are Jeffries Lagheart the man that's supposed to take over Manhattan." Then two men dragged that body to a building and left.

"Hey Ted what are we going to do with him?" asked Baker. "It took us a while to catch up with Jeffries Lagheart but I'm more than sure that he's the one."

"Well good bring him to the warehouse. I've got some business to settle with him." replied Ted Manhattan. "Holmes I hear has fallen for someone's trap. He gone on a wild goose chase for gold."

Ted then hung his phone up. He'd decided that whoever was working with Jeffries Lagheart, had to have know pretty much about Ted's personal business. Darn it who could it had been. It began to worry Ted. He'd get that best info that he could about them then he'd make a decision what to do afterwards. Sure Ted was nice but sometime you have to do what you have to do.

"You sure that that's Jeffries Lagheart?" asked Ted Manhattan. "Now we've got the other one to catch, ok Baker."

"Ok Ted I got you. Heading for you now." replied Baker. "Hey I get big pay for this don't I?"

"Good hurry because I don't feel like we've got too much time."

"Repeat that Ted I didn't hear you your phone is breaking up." responded Baker. "Hurry because... we ain't"

"Got too much time Baker!"

"Ok, ok , ok." exclaimed Baker. "On the way."

Ted headed towards his bedroom. Karen Manhattan had an expression on her face as if she'd found herself confused. She was now at the urged of asking Ted just what was on his mind.

"Ted, what's going on?" she asked with a bit of confusion.

"Karen just going out to take care of some business." said Ted Manhattan. "Well as you know you know our daughter's out there somewhere and who knows what could be happening."

"What's your point Ted?"

"I'm going out there to find our daughter." replied Ted. "I'm going to bring her home."

Karen hung her head down she'd already lost her daughter seemly. Could this be a message saying that she'd be missing her husband too. She knelt down on her knees and began to pray. Jesus would deliver her, Surely he was the answer.

"Karen don't worry I'll be back." he said. " And I'll bring our daughter back too."

"Ted you never disappointed me before, remember. Don't let me down now." she said with a tear in her eye. "Oh my perious darlin."

"Just take care of home until I come back ok?" said Ted.

"Well Ted you just hurry back."

Karen was no fool Ted was up to something, Sure he love his daughter just as she did, but he felt betryal somewhere down the line. Martha was smart. Ted was beginning to catch on now, there was talk and signs around town saying that this queen was going to be Master of Manhattan, her and her man and no one could stop them. Well it was obvious to Ted tha t the legacy was supposed to have been passed down to Martha. It was plain understood to everyone in Manhattan. Ted Manhattan then got into his car.

"Well looks like it's back to the old days." said Ted as he brought out something that he could never let no one else see. "The Lady Dance With Me. The one who save my life many times back in the days. If I'm going to go out I'm going to go out with you in my hand." He then started his car. "Now shall we dance?"

Ted cruised down the street. His 2007 Mesedez had flashers blinking. Since he rarely drove it. No one know who he was.

Then his cellar phone rung. "Hello, this is Ted Manhattan speaking."

"Ted this is Baker, I just had to let you know that, I can't make it to the warehouse."

"Why Baker?" Ted demanded an explanation.

"Because some man by the name of Janu Ed Valezque followed me into the warehouse and tied me up."

"Danm it it Baker you are supposed to be my main hit man. And you let something like this happed.?" said Ted Manhattan in anger. "How many there?"

"Two."

" What do they look like?" asked Ted Manhattan. As to be angry.

"One male and the other female." replied Baker.,

"Those Bastards ," said Ted Manhattan. "They recked my crew."

Ted began to find hi s way to the warehouse. He had three more blocks to go. The lady the dance was right be side him. He couldn't drive to the front door of the warehouse that would make things a little too suspicious. He'd have to walk that alley. It was the only way of his and Baker chance of survival.

"Let him go."

"We figured you'd sneak in here Ted." said one of the gun holders. "But by no means are we going to let Baker, here go. Think about it Ted he's your main hit man. He'd track us down at anytime."

"I said let him go."

"What do we get out of this?" asked the female.

"What'cha want?" asked Ted Manhattan.

"Say the city of Manhattan?" the gun holder said.

"Hey what are you going to do?" asked the female. "You know we ain't got too much time to waste."

Ted thought a moment how about half the city? He could do that much for Baker. Heck he'd known him a long time. But there was no chance that two strangers could convince Ted Manhattan into turning over his city to them. Sure Baker was his main hit man but. Ted had to rule Ted had to show the world how powerful he was, it was never again stand a chance of anyone trying to take it away from his family.

"Baker?"

"Yes, Ted, boss?"

""Tell me are you all right?" asked Ted. "At least say something."

"I'm ok Boss." replied Baker as reassurance. "Hey it's just like old times. I see that you've got the Lady Dance With Me by your side."

"I do." responded Ted.

"Good because you might be the only one getting out of here alive." said Baker as to be in pain as to have been pistol wiped. "Man it been..."

Before Baker was too soon gone. It wasn't the gunman

and the female that shot Baker. It was someone from the roof, Ted then took off running he had to find out who shot Baker. When found he was going to hang them.

"Hold it Ted." said a voice from the roof. "Manhattan belongs to me this day."

Then the stranger ran and jumped. Ted had to catch him. He'd shot Ted's main hit man. Ted was not worried about the shooter getting away. He knew all the passages but the stranger did not. Then there was another voice.

"Hold Ted Manhattan freeze ." said the female. "We're not through talking yet."

"Oh yes we are." replied Ted Manhattan. "Someone just shot my main hit man. So you can say what you want but I'm gone."

No one knew the passages to the warehouse like Ted. In no time no one knew where he was. It was a long run for the shooter but a short run for Ted. "Hold it right there Mr."

"Ok, you got me." said the Shooter. "Did I kill em'?"

"You damn right you did." exclaimed Ted. "Baker oh poor Baker was my main hit man."

"Is there anyway that you could forgive me?"

"Forgive you?" said Ted Manhattan in great anger. "For shooting my best hit man." Then Ted shot one time at the shooter's feet. "No damn you."

The shooter then jumped from a box. "You know." said the shooter. "I know lik e you know this room contains explosives. You can't not shoot a gun in here."

"Damn," said Ted. "He's right. I'll later blow the whole building up."

Ted ran and jumped. He had to see who it was that

killed Baker. It they'd gotten away this time he'd later never find out who it was, then those two who held him up before the stranger shot Baker, must had ben pretty experienced about Manhattan.Ted found himself using stragtergies. He'd use his voice to catch the strangers attention.

"Hey Mr. You'd never get away you'd better give up now." said Ted Manhattan. "Know that you have a hard ways to go in here I designed it so no one would know this warehouse like myself, so stop your running there Mr."

The stranger then turned around.

""Joe... Joe Holmes." said Ted with a shock. "I thought you'd left the country."

"Come on Ted did you really expect me to go on some wild gold chase. Now think about that thing, this is Joe Holmes."

"Well you didn't leave the country?" asked Ted as to felt lost. "But three week ago you did convince Martha my daughter to leave home?"

"I did."

"What did you say?" replied Ted.

" I made a bargain with her." said Joe Holmes.

"Yeah, go on."

"Half and Half." responded Joe Holmes.

"You mean..."

"Yeah, Martha met a man named Jeffries Lagheart, we were all in for the prize of Manhattan NY." said Joe Holmes.

"Well shot me dead." said Ted Manhattan as not to be a bit of surprized at Joe Holmes. "My very daughter doubled crossed me."

"That's right now you see how good I look before the ladies?"

"Yeah dam right I do. So what happens from here?" sighed Ted. "You're dead Ted Manhattan?"

Then Ted used his good ear. He'd hear people talking down below. He had to out smart Joe Holmes for once. "Here take my gun. Now you have both guns. Now when you get on the very top of the forth of the roof. Wave my gun continuously.

That's all I ask. Ok?"

"Ok, that's the least I can do for a dead man"

Joe Holmes did not kn ow that people was looking for Ted Manhattan's gun and if waved in the night it would glow. Joe Holmes was about to get shot and didn't even know.

Then Ted said, "Ready?"

"Yeah," said Joe Holmes as he wagged his gun, "Let's get going I ain't got all day."

Joe Holmes did just as Ted said when they'd reached the top. At no time guns began to fire. Holmes fired only one into the air before he'd fallen face flat to the ground. With the Lady that Dance in his hand. Martha was a bit bitter but she'd did it. She couldn't turn the body over. She couldn't face seeing her Father, Ted Manhattan laying there.

Then Martha said, "Let's go."

"You're going to leave your Father there like that?" asked Jeffries. Lagheart. "At least we could..."

"No I said let's go."

"You go." said Jeffries as to be disappointed in Martha. "I'm taking your father's body with me."

"Well if you insist come on."

"Good people ," said Ted as he left the roof. Headed towards his home. Martha didn't know it but she was going to meet a surprize. "Ted was alive."

He hopped into his 2007 Mesedez. This was one of the few of the top name brand cars. It had a blue color. With red lights that continuously said the Manhattans. Ted felt proud, who could had pulled off something like that besides him? Ted Manhattan? He then got on his phone and called his wife. "Hello, Karen , hon I'm on my way home."

"Well good bring our daughter as you said there Ted." she ordered him. "And don't let it take you too long because I have not seen my daughter in ages, Ted Manhattan."

"Karen, Karen, now didn't I tell you that I was going to bring our daughter home?"

"You did." she said as to hold him to his promise.

"Well when I get there she'd be there also."

"How do you know Ted?" replied Karen. "Is she with you?"

"Karen I will have you to know that I have had my daughter tracked every since the day she was born, ok?" said Ted as to get tied of he questions. "Now I damn well take care of my daughter Karen Manhattan."

She was stunned. She never heard him speak so angrily. He meant business. And he was bound to find who ever he was after. Either they'd surrender or he'd find them.

"Ok, Ted dear I hear you."

"Well good Karen darlin'" responded Ted Manhattan.

He then hung his phone up. He was headed for home now. As he turned on his radio he could hear it state a possible blackout. He paid little attention to it. He was all but worried now, for he was the greatest man in Manhattan.

Ted thought, to himself. Had he been a little to hard on Karen. Sure he was Ted Manhattan, and he'd owned the city of Manhattan. But Karen was his wife, what would he do if he'd lost her? It just would not be the same without her. He decided to call her back and apolgize.

Karen answered the phone

"Karen," said Ted. "Hon I just called back to appologize. Are you ok. Because I surely love you dear."

"Oh Ted you honey bun you."

"Just wanted to remind you how much I care." exclaimed Ted.

"Well hon glad that you called." replied Karen.

"Sure thing be home soon."

He then lit a cigerette. Ted was about to stop for a drink but then he decide that he'd promised Karen that he was coming right over. So he kept going. He appreciated a woman like Karen. She was always nice and kind.

"Ted?" said Karen with passion. "I love you too."

It was not long before Martha had reached her Mother. She folded her hands and told her Mother that she had bad news.

"What's the bad news Martha?" asked Karen.

"Well it's about Father, Mother and it hard for me to tell."

Ted walked in the back door, "Tell it Martha, your dear Mother and I are waiting to hear just what you have to say"

Martha was stunned. There he was, Ted Manhattan. Six one, brown skin, and a smile that could not be made straight.

"Father?"

"Yes, Martha?" said Ted as to love his daughter and be angry at her at the same time. "Don't know what to say. Please forgive me Father."

"I will once you explain this reasoning?"

"Ok I made a bargain with Joe Holmes." she sighed as wanting pity. "Ok I want Jeffries and I to be Master of Manhattan."

"And?"

"Sooner or later we were going to double cross Joe Holmes." replied Martha.

"And knowing you Martha, you were going to double cross Jeffries somewhere down the line." stated Ted Manhattan.

"Is this true Martha?" asked Jeffries Lagheart.

"I'm I telling the truth Martha?"

"Yes, Jeffries that's where that old lady that you met on the subway came in, and that same old lady that followed you, we made a bargain."

"A bargain?" asked Jeffries as to be very disappointed. "What's her name?"

"I don't know I met the homeless at a bus stop one day although I'm never going to be homeless, and I going to be rich. I did give her $5,000.00, to carry out my plans."

"So you used us all?" asked her Father. "Darn after all...."

"Not so fast Ted, she didn't use us all. I'm that old lady."

"What?" he replied.

"Now I knew that the family was falling apart so I kept track of every move of our daughter Martha, there Ted." said Karen. "I couldn't be two places at one time so I faked the sickness, and had my twin sister yes we look exactly alike."

"Mother?"

"Karen?" said Ted. "What's going on?"

Then there was a loud knock on the door. No one at the

Manhattan's suspected it. It was the police. The chief of the squad said, "I find you guilty of murder Ted Manhattan."

"What? I killed no one."

"Well good come and prove that in the court of justice." said the chief of the squad.

"Where are you taking my husband?" Said Karen with excitement.

"Just get me out Karen, don't let them keep me in there, ok hon?"

Then it was just like it had been broadcasted, there was a black out. Martha then found her self grabbing Jeffries', Karen's, and Ted's hands and escaping thru a passage in the house there no one knew but her.

There was a struggle but the police was among themselves. At that moment Martha knew that she had a man that loved her. She knew that love could be blind a lesson that she'd taught Jeffries Legheart. He may or he may never struggle with what she put him thru. But one thing was for sure is that she love him too.

The passage door closed. And Martha said, "We're out of here." They were gone and then the lights came back on. Martha will always be, ***MASTER OF MANHATTAN.***